Amee-nah

Amazing Indian Children series

Amee-nah

Zuni Boy Runs the Race of His Life

Kenneth
Thomasma

Jack Brouwer
Illustrator

Grandview Publishing Company
Box 2863, Jackson, WY 83001

Published by Grandview Publishing Company,
Box 2863, Jackson, WY 83001

Second printing, October 1998
Third printing, August 2001

Printed in the United States of America

ISBN: 1-880114-17-8 (Grandview Publishing Company)
ISBN: 1-880114-15-1 (Grandview Publishing Company; pbk.)

**Special thanks
to:**

Al Kuipers
retired educator and friend

**Zuni elders
John Charles Cheama and Paul Neha**
The staff of Zuni Christian School
Zuni, New Mexico

Wendell Brown
Executive Director, Orthopaedics
of Jackson Hole

Larry Van Genderen
orthopedic surgeon and longtime friend

**The boys and girls of Kelly School
Kelly, Wyoming**

Contents

Preface

In 1952 I was employed as a summer camp counselor at Camp Manitou-lin near Middleville, Michigan. I was a rookie counselor between my junior and senior years at Calvin College in Grand Rapids, Michigan.

At an evening campfire, veteran counselor, Al Kuipers, told the campers a stirring story about a Zuni Indian boy. The story of this boy's courage and determination to overcome a severe handicap stayed with me. I would retell the story many times in my future work in summer camps and during my career as a teacher.

Forty-two years later in 1994, I learned that Al
Kuipers was living in retirement in Sandy, Utah, just
five hours from our home in Jackson Hole,
Wyoming. I contacted Al and his wife, Barbara.
While visiting Jackson Hole, they stopped in for a
visit. I asked Al if he would mind my using his story
as the seed for a book about the Zuni boy. He
thought it was a great idea and offered to help in
anyway he could. While his parents were missionar-
ies to the Zuni people, Al had collected many books
and much knowledge about the Zuni.

The writing of Amee-nah's story required
research into the birth defect called clubfoot. I had
to learn all the details of the unique stickraces com-
peted in by young men and boys. I carefully
inspected the terrain around the Zuni Pueblo and
visited places where the sheep camps were located.

Two Zuni elders were a great help during my visits to Zuni. John Charles "J. C." Cheama showed me
around the Zuni area. He shared his firsthand
knowledge of his people and their homeland. Paul
Neha was the stickrace expert. In his youth Paul

actually ran in stickraces. Stickracing ended in the 1940s. Paul showed me a real stick used in these grueling twenty-five-mile races. He still carries a stick under the seat in his pickup truck. Zuni Christian School teachers and staff did everything they could to assist me and put me in touch with Paul and J. C.

Everywhere we went in the Zuni Pueblo my wife, Bobbi, and I were treated warmly by the friendly Zuni. We were impressed by the furniture being manufactured by the Zuni people in their own factory in Blackrock and now own several beautiful pieces. We also have some beautiful Zuni jewelry obtained directly from the artists.

The Zuni people are a proud tribe and maintain close family ties and traditions. They have served valiantly in our country's wars, and continue to provide crack forest firefighters who serve all over the U.S.A.

Amee-nah is a fictional story based on the life of a boy who actually lived.

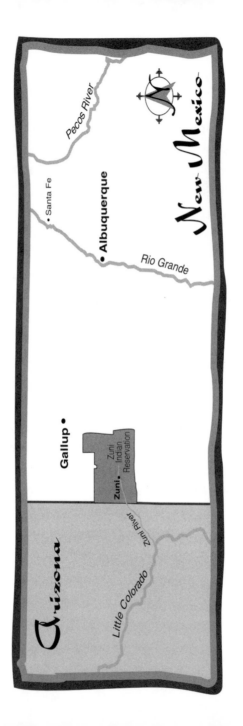

1

A Critical Decision

The March days of 1939 were getting longer. Every day the sun was a little higher in the blue New Mexico sky. School had just let out for the day. The Zuni village (called a pueblo) was full of kids on their way home from school. One Zuni boy limped along toward his home as he had done all of the ten years of his life. Amee-nah hated to see summer come. It meant all the other boys would be leaving for sheep camp. Amee-nah would be left behind.

The name Amee-nah was given this ten-year-old by a few other boys his age. Nathan was his real name. In Zuni Amee-nah means "lazy." The others called him lazy because he never went to sheep camp. He never ran in the stick races. He never played any games with the other boys.

Amee-nah was always careful to keep his right foot hidden. Every night before climbing into bed the boy would sit and stare at his foot. He hated the ugly sight of his twisted foot, which was crooked and turned under. He was born with the deformed foot called clubfoot.

Why did he have to have such a foot? No one else had an ugly foot like his. Why did he have to limp? The boy could never find answers to these questions.

Amee-nah was different for another reason. He did not have a father. His father had been a forest firefighter. Zuni men are some of the best firefighters in all of America. When Amee-nah was three years old, his father was killed in a fire far from the Zuni pueblo. The tragedy happened up north in Colorado.

Amee-nah was eight years old when he finally heard the whole story of his father's death. A dangerous forest fire had started high in the Colorado mountains. A special team of Zuni firefighters was brought in to keep the advancing fire from crossing a mountain ridge. If the fire was not stopped before topping the ridge, many homes in the next valley would be destroyed.

Amee-nah's father and his fellow Zuni firefighters fought the blaze for thirty-six straight hours without even a short rest. They thought they had won the battle and were almost ready to turn the mop-up work over to other crews. Suddenly and without warning a violent wind roared out of a canyon above the men. It sent the fire into a raging flare-up.

The wall of flames turned on the Zuni men as they raced for their lives toward a nearby mountain lake. In the frantic dash for safety one man stumbled and fell. He lay in the rocks with a broken hip. Amee-nah's father nearly tripped over his friend who had fallen in front of him. The boy's father stopped and lifted the injured man onto his sturdy shoulders.

The small lake was only three hundred feet away. The other Zuni men had not seen the accident. They were already diving into the water. The men looked around to see if everyone had made it. To their horror they saw Amee-nah's father running with the injured man over his shoulders. The two men didn't have a chance. The wall of flames engulfed them. There was nothing the other men could do but stand and witness the instant deaths of their two friends.

Eight-year-old Amee-nah sat next to his mother and listened as a man told the story of this hero's death. After the story, he watched as a United States Forest Service ranger gave his mother a beautiful medal. In telling the story the ranger had used some big words that the boy didn't understand. He did know that it was exactly five years ago that his father had given his life trying to save a fallen friend. He did know that his father could have left the man and saved himself.

When the ranger gave Amee-nah's mother the medal, over three hundred people who had listened in utter silence all stood and clapped. The clapping went on and on. It was so loud that it could be heard all over the streets of the Zuni pueblo. Even now, at age ten, Amee-nah could still hear the clapping in his mind. He knew he had had a very special father. It was Amee-nah's dream to someday be a firefighter like his father had been. This made him hate his twisted foot even more. He could never be a firefighter if he was only able to limp along all of his life.

Amee-nah had no brothers or sisters. He knew he was the only one who could grow up to be brave like his father. He made up his mind to find a way to make his mother proud of him.

On this day after school Amee-nah was almost home when he saw Mawee running toward him. Mawee was one of the fastest runners in the whole pueblo. He was also the only boy who paid any attention to Amee-nah. Something had made Mawee different from the rest of the kids.

"Hey, wait for me!" Mawee yelled.

"Hi, Mawee! What's going on?" answered Amee-nah.

"We have another injured lamb. It was attacked by a bunch of ravens. They tried to peck out the eyes. That's how they make a lamb helpless so it will die and become a meal for the hungry birds. The lamb will die if someone doesn't take care of it. You helped two other lambs whose mothers were killed. How about taking care of another one?"

"Is it blind?" Amee-nah asked.

"We don't know how bad the eyes are. Right now it can't see, but my dad says maybe the eyes will heal," Mawee explained.

"Sure, I'll take it. Bring it over anytime," Amee-nah offered.

"Thanks! I didn't want to leave it for the ravens to finish or the coyotes and bobcats to find. Hey, how about going to sheep camp this summer?" Mawee suggested.

"No. No, thanks. I wouldn't be much good there. I'm no good at running," Amee-nah muttered.

"Hey, Amee-nah, you can do it. Every day we run the hillsides to check on the sheep. We are on the lookout for wolves, bobcats, and any danger that might trouble the sheep. I can run the upper part of the hills. You can cover the lower places. Your route will be shorter. Sheep camp is a blast. We have our own stone shelter, cook our own food, and have a campfire every night. Come on. Try it just once. You'll love it. Maybe your limp will go away," Mawee said as he turned to leave.

"I'll think about it. Maybe someday I can go," Amee-nah mumbled as he headed home.

The boy was still getting used to going through the new door in his house. The new entry had been cut into their old-style home only two weeks before. Amee-nah and his mother had climbed a ladder and went through an opening in the roof before they had the door. In the old days the ladder could be pulled up so no one could enter. It was a way to protect a family from their enemy warriors. Many years before peace had come to all Indian people. Indian raids and wars were a thing of the past.

Amee-nah's mother had bread baking in an outside oven as the Zuni still do today. She was busy grinding corn into cornmeal. On one side of the large room several clay pots were drying on a table. The boy's mother was an expert pottery maker. Her beautiful pieces of pottery were sold to tourists to make enough money for the two of them to live.

"Hi, son. I'm glad you're home. Go out and take the bread out of the oven. We'll eat it for supper," Amee-nah's mother said.

"Mom, Mawee has another lamb for me to take care of. It might be blind. Some ravens attacked it and hurt its eyes."

"Ravens can be dangerous when they're hungry. If the lamb is blind, you'll have to watch it all the time. It will be helpless. You'll have to feed it with a baby bottle and keep it inside at night. You're good with animals. They know you love them. They trust you."

After Amee-nah finished supper, Mawee came over with the injured lamb. Amee-nah took the helpless lamb in his arms. The little one's eyes looked horrible. The eyeballs were swollen and bleeding. The lamb trembled and made a tiny bleating sound.

The boy held the little lamb gently and quietly talked to it. He found a soft piece of cloth and dipped it in warm water. Amee-nah slowly laid the cloth over the animal's injured eyes.

The startled lamb squirmed in the boy's arms for a few short seconds. Amee-nah held the lamb firmly and continued to talk to it. In less than a minute the animal began to relax. It seemed to understand that the boy was trying to help.

As the days passed, Amee-nah spent every free minute with the lamb. He continued to bathe the lamb's eyes, and the left eye that was not as badly injured began to heal. The other eye did not seem to heal well. He was sure the lamb would never see out of that eye. The left eye was the poor lamb's only chance ever to see again.

Eleven days after Mawee had dropped off the lamb at Amee-nah's house, he came back to check on the injured animal. Amee-nah was on his way home from the public school. Mawee had just started going to the mission school last fall. The two boys met not far from Amee-nah's house. A surprise was waiting for them as they walked along and talked about the lamb's condition. Mawee was the first to see the amazing sight.

"Look, Amee-nah! The lamb is coming out of your house. Your mom let it out!" Mawee cried.

"Stop, Mawee! I think the lamb can see. It's coming toward us! It can see!" blurted Amee-nah.

"Shhh! Don't make a sound. Maybe it just hears us. Follow me. We'll find out if it can really see or not," Mawee whispered.

The two boys moved sharply to the right. The lamb turned toward them. Next they moved back to the left on their tiptoes. Again the lamb changed direction and came toward them.

"It can see!" Mawee shouted. "Amee-nah, you did it! This is great! Look, the lamb knows you! It's coming right at you! This is great. The lamb can see!"

Amee-nah reached down and picked up the small animal. The good eye looked clearer than ever. It seemed to move back and forth even better than even the day before.

"Son, I let the lamb out when I saw you coming. It has been walking around without any trouble. As soon as you left for school, I noticed how well the lamb was walking. I'm sure the lamb can see with its good eye."

Amee-nah felt like singing. The one-eyed lamb felt so soft and warm in the boy's arms. Now it could see. Someday the lamb could return to the flock and live a normal life.

Mawee reached over and rubbed the lamb's head. "Amee-nah, you have to go to sheep camp with me. You are great with animals. We always have sheep that need special help. You would love sheep camp. It's a blast. You could do a lot of good," Mawee babbled with excitement.

"I'll see what my mother says," Amee-nah answered, trying to avoid saying yes or no.

"Also, Amee-nah, my teacher at the mission school wants to see your foot. I told him about you and he thinks he knows what's wrong. He thinks it can be fixed. How soon can you come to my school to let him see your foot? He's there every day for two hours after school. How about it?"

Mawee's words shocked Amee-nah. He stood there like a statue. See my foot? Maybe it can be fixed? These ideas paralyzed Amee-nah. Did Mawee really say those words? With a confused look Amee-nah replied, "I'll see what my mother says."

"Okay! But you have to give me an answer tomorrow!" hollered Mawee as he walked away.

With the little lamb in his arms, Amee-nah felt light-headed as he walked the short distance to his door. The boy softly stroked the woolly lamb. The lamb can see. Mawee wants me to show my foot to his teacher. Maybe my foot can be fixed. The boy was ashamed of his ugly foot and never wanted anyone, especially not a stranger, to see it. These thoughts raced around in Amee-nah's head causing him to feel dizzy.

Let Mawee know in the morning. How could he decide that soon? Amee-nah hardly heard anything his mother said to him that night. She had to repeat everything before her son responded. She knew something was bothering him. In time she knew her son would tell her what troubled him.

What would Amee-nah tell his friend? He could not decide. He would have trouble going to sleep as he desperately tried to make up his mind. He had no way of knowing that his decision would come to him in the middle of the night in an amazing way. Before morning he would know exactly what he would tell Mawee.

2

A Dramatic Answer

After Amee-nah ate his supper, he fed the little lamb a bottle of milk. The tiny animal took the nipple as eagerly as any human baby. The boy stroked the lamb's woolly coat. He noticed the lamb's bad eye blinked often. The eyeball still appeared badly damaged. It was swollen and discolored.

As soon as the lamb emptied the bottle, Amee-nah dipped a cloth in warm water and held it gently over the injured eye. The woolly infant squirmed a little before relaxing.

"Good lamb, Blinky," the boy whispered. "Blinky, yes, that's a perfect name for you, little one. Blinky you are."

Amee-nah continued to dip the soft cloth in the warm water and hold it to the lamb's eye. The boy's mother was talking to his uncle, James, who had stopped by to check on her and her son. Uncle James was married to Amee-nah's mother's sister. Zuni relatives still live near each other as they did in the old days. Uncle James was like a father to Amee-nah. He always made sure everything was okay for his nephew and sister-in-law.

That night Amee-nah and Blinky lay side by side in the boy's bed. Moonlight came in through the window. Amee-nah stared out at the moon as thin clouds passed in front of the brilliant light. The clouds seemed like gentle waves rolling through the night sky.

Amee-nah began to think about everything that had happened that day. He smiled when he remembered how Blinky came walking up to him and Mawee proving he could see out of his good eye. He felt good about being able to help the tiny animal.

When Amee-nah thought about Mawee's words his heart beat a little faster. "My teacher wants to see your foot. He thinks your foot can be fixed." Amee-nah had never let anyone see his foot. He was ashamed of it. He even thought there might be some unknown reason that he had to have a crippled foot.

What should I do? Amee-nah thought. *What am I going to tell Mawee? How could my foot be fixed? Could it really be done? Could I ever walk and run like other kids? What should I do? What should I say to Mawee?*

Amee-nah lay awake for over two hours without deciding what to do. When he finally fell asleep, he was very restless. Just before dawn Amee-nah began dreaming. In his dream he saw his father running through a forest. He saw his father stop to pick up a fallen person. Like an explosion, trees instantly burst into flames.

Next Amee-nah felt his father picking him up. The boy was being rescued by his own father. The heat was scorching hot. There it was, a lake, straight ahead.

Silently Amee-nah's father ran with the boy over his shoulders. Suddenly Amee-nah saw men standing in the lake. They were all clapping. Then Amee-nah saw a boy in the water. It was Mawee! He was clapping more loudly than anyone else. The clapping became louder and louder. Instantly everything changed. Amee-nah himself was running. His father had just disappeared. The boy was running with his limp gone and at a great speed.

The last thing Amee-nah remembered was the loud clapping. The dream ended before Amee-nah reached the lake. He woke up sweating. His dream seemed real.

The sun was up. Sunlight poured through the bedroom window. Amee-nah looked out at the bright blue sky. Never had the sky seemed bluer. *I have my answer,* the boy said to himself. *The clapping in my dream is the answer. I do want to run like*

Mawee. I do want my foot to be fixed. Right after school I'll tell Mawee I'll let his teacher see my foot.

Amee-nah practically jumped out of bed. He fed Blinky, ate his own breakfast, and headed off to school. In his excitement Amee-nah forgot to tell his mother about his decision. Halfway to school he realized he should have talked his plans over with his mother. As soon as school let out, he would head for home to talk to her.

Only one block from his house, Amee-nah spotted Mawee at the next corner. "Mawee! Wait up," yelled Amee-nah.

Mawee stopped and turned to see Amee-nah running toward him limp and all. Mawee saw the smile on Amee-nah's face. "Amee-nah! You're smiling. You've decided to let my teacher see your foot! That's great!" Mawee blurted.

"Mawee, you won't believe this! I had a dream. My dad was in it. He was saving me from a forest fire. Then he disappeared, and I was running by myself. My limp was gone. You were in my dream clapping for me. Maybe my foot can be fixed.

Maybe someday I can run like my dad could. Maybe someday I can run like you can."

Mawee put his arm on Amee-nah's shoulder. "Hey, you will run. You'll be great. You'll probably beat me someday. Nobody will call you Amee-nah anymore. They'll call you Mawee the Second. I'll tell my teacher. We'll see you after school."

The two friends parted. Mawee headed off to the mission school, and Amee-nah limped off to his school.

That day in school Amee-nah had a hard time paying attention to his teacher. Every few minutes he glanced at the clock. Time seemed to drag slowly. Amee-nah's teacher finally asked him if anything was wrong. After the boy told his teacher nothing was wrong, he did his best to pay more attention and to try not to look at the clock.

Finally the school day ended. Amee-nah headed home to talk to his mother. He hardly noticed anything around him on his way home. All the excited boy could think about was his visit to Mawee's teacher at the mission school. He kept looking down at his foot still hidden from view in his oversized shoe. He thought about the moment coming very soon when he would take the shoe off and let the teacher see it. This day could change Ameenah's life forever.

The boy's mother was outside taking clothes off the clothesline where they were hung today. She saw her son coming around the corner and met him at the door.

"Son, I had a visitor today. Coach K from the mission school came to tell me about your visit to his school. He asked me if it was all right for him to have a look at your foot."

"Mom, I forgot to tell you about it. That's why I came home right away. Mawee talked me into doing it."

"Son, I like Coach K. I know he wants to help you. Are you going to see him?"

"I want to, Mom, if it's okay with you."

"I hope you do it. I want my boy to be happy. I'm sure Coach K wants to do what's best for you. I hope you go see him. I already fed Blinky for you. He can stay in his pen. Hurry back and tell me what happened."

"I will, Mom. Thanks."

Amee-nah turned and hurried off toward Mawee's school. He felt even happier now after finding out his mother thought he was doing the right thing. With each step he took, Amee-nah became more excited. He had a good feeling inside. He couldn't wait to meet Coach K and show him his twisted foot. Something inside told him something great was about to happen.

Amee-nah had not been to Mawee's school before. He was almost there when Mawee saw him coming. Mawee raced over to Amee-nah.

"Amee-nah! Boy, am I glad to see you! Coach K is in a meeting. He'll be done in about fifteen minutes. He told me to tell you he's sorry to keep you waiting."

"That's okay. I'll wait all afternoon if I have to. I'm ready to let him see this stupid foot of mine. I even want you to see it. Now you'll know why I hate what it looks like."

Mawee had Amee-nah tell him again about his dream. Before he could finish the story of the dream, Coach K opened the door and came out of his meeting.

"Hi, Amee-nah. I'm Coach K. I'm really glad you came. Mawee is a good friend. He told me how good you are with animals. Sounds like you might be a veterinarian someday. Come on in. We'll take a look at that foot."

Amee-nah liked Coach K's voice. He seemed calm and very kind. The boy felt at ease and followed the teacher into the school.

Coach K walked into a room which had a small bed along one wall. There was a desk opposite the bed. Two chairs stood near the desk.

"Here we are, Amee-nah. Have a seat on the edge of the bed. Okay if Mawee stays?"

"Sure is. He's my best friend. If it wasn't for him, I wouldn't be here," Amee-nah replied as he smiled at the teacher.

Mawee looked right at Amee-nah. Both boys were smiling. As the two boys' eyes met, Amee-nah knew he really did have a true friend. He was ready for anything. He could still hear the clapping from his dream.

Amee-nah loosened the shoelaces. He pulled the old shoe off. His stocking came off with it. Mawee was shocked at the sight of the grotesque foot. Amee-nah noticed Mawee's shocked expression.

"I told you it's ugly. Now you know for sure," Amee-nah said.

Coach K examined Amee-nah's foot carefully. He raised it up to see it from every possible angle. No one spoke. Amee-nah realized he was holding his breath. He was becoming tense with excitement and worry. At last Coach K spoke. "Amee-nah, do you know what doctors call a foot like yours?"

"No, I don't," Amee-nah answered nervously.

"It's called a clubfoot. It happened before you were born. Your foot grew this way. Other people have been born with a clubfoot. The good news is, it can be fixed. Your foot is not as bad as some. It could be much worse."

Coach K's words caused Amee-nah's heart to beat faster. "My foot can be fixed?" The boy didn't know what else to say.

"Amee-nah! Isn't that great!" blurted Mawee. "I knew it! I just knew it! They can make your foot as good as new. You'll be a runner. Sheep camp, here we come!"

"Hold on, Mawee. This is up to Amee-nah. He has to decide what to do. He'll need his mother's permission. This will all take time," Coach K cautioned.

"What needs to be done to my foot? How can they fix it?" Amee-nah asked.

"First, you'll have to see a doctor. The doctor will explain everything to you and your mother. You will need surgery. You'll need to learn to walk all over again. It won't be easy, but it can be done, that's for sure," explained Coach K. "Talk to your mother. Have her come to see me. We'll figure out what to do next."

"Thanks, Coach. I'll talk to my mom and my Uncle James right away," Amee-nah promised excitedly.

Amee-nah pulled his sock and shoe back over the twisted foot, stood up, thanked Coach K again, and headed out of the building with Mawee. The two boys jabbered away as they turned toward Amee-nah's house.

"Wasn't that great news, Amee-nah? Coach K is a super teacher. He really cares about us kids," Mawee said with pride.

"What's really great is he cares about me, too. I wonder what my mom will say. I know she'll talk to Uncle James. Now I can't wait to find out what the doctor will say," Amee-nah thought out loud.

The answers that waited for the boy who limped would come quickly. One answer would sadden him. Other answers would be unbelievable. One thing was sure, Amee-nah's life would never be the same after this dramatic day.

3

Be Patient

Amee-nah hardly noticed anyone or anything on his way home. He walked through the door and blurted out to his mother, "Mom, my foot can be fixed. Coach K says my foot can be fixed. He says I need surgery."

"That's wonderful, son. I was hoping he would say that, but, son, don't get too excited. Remember, surgery costs lots of money. We don't have much money. Somehow I'll find a way to borrow the money. It might take time to get a loan. You'll have to be patient."

At first Amee-nah was confused. Then he felt a huge letdown. He had not thought about cost. The only thing he thought about was being able to walk and run like the other kids. Now he realized he would be causing his mother to face a big problem. She would have to borrow lots of money and work for years to pay it back. He couldn't make her do that.

Amee-nah's smile was gone. Silently he ambled over to Blinky's pen. He reached down and scooped up the lamb. His mother handed him the lamb's baby bottle. She put her hand on her son's shoulder. "Son, don't worry about the money. Whatever it costs will be worth it. It will all work out. You'll see."

Blinky gulped down the milk in no time. Amee-nah sat in the corner holding the bundle of wool. He gently stroked the lamb as he sat in deep thought. He wondered about how fast his excitement and happiness had turned to confusion and disappointment. How much would an operation cost? How long would it take his mother to pay for it? The boy had no way of knowing about the costs of operations. He only knew his mother had very little money for extras.

That night Amee-nah went to bed early. He lay awake for a long time thinking. He remembered Coach K's exciting words, "Your foot can be fixed."

"Nuts, why didn't I ask Coach how much an operation would cost? I wish I would have thought to ask him some questions. I just can't make my mother work day and night to pay for surgery on my stupid foot."

Amee-nah finally fell asleep. He planned to get up early and go see Coach K before school to get some more answers. The boy didn't know that the next day would be almost as exciting as the day he just finished. Coach K would have another fantastic surprise for the boy who limped. Something that had happened years before and hundreds of miles away would now affect this Zuni boy's future.

Amee-nah was so tired from not having been able to fall asleep the last two nights that he overslept.

No time to see Coach K before school now. The boy
fed Blinky, gulped down his breakfast, and left for
school. His mother had been up for two hours
working on her pottery; Amee-nah said nothing
more to her about his foot and an operation. That
night he would tell her he had changed his mind
and didn't want to suffer the pain of an operation.

Amee-nah caught himself daydreaming in school
that day. He had to force himself to pay attention to
his teacher and his work. The day dragged on and
was almost over when the principal walked into
Amee-nah's classroom. He handed the teacher a
note and left. The boy's teacher read the note,
walked back to Amee-nah's desk, and laid it in front
of him. The words on the note seemed to jump out
at the boy.

"After school, go to the mission school. Your
mother will meet you there."

*My mother will meet me at Mawee's school? Why?
He had just been there the day before. Why did they
want him to come back so soon? Why do they want
my mother to be there? It must have something to do*

with my old twisted foot. I know. They're going to tell us how much the operation will cost. I don't even want to know. I know it will be way too much, Amee-nah decided.

The boy was so lost in thought he did not hear the bell. When all the other kids jumped up to leave, Amee-nah grabbed his books and headed out. He limped along still wondering what was going to happen next. As he rounded the final corner and saw the mission school ahead, he caught sight of a figure running full speed toward him.

"Amee-nah!" Mawee shouted. "Hurry up! Your mother is already here!"

In no time Mawee was at Amee-nah's side. Mawee was such a strong runner that he was hardly out of breath.

"Mawee, what's going on? Why is my mother here? What's happening? Don't tell me Coach K needs to see my foot again."

"Hey, I'm not telling. Boy, are you going to be surprised today! Come on. Let's get in there." Mawee teased.

The two friends walked side by side to the mission school. Amee-nah was bewildered. Why was Mawee so excited? The way his friend acted, Amee-nah knew something special was about to happen. What could it be?

Coach K met Mawee and Amee-nah at the door and let them into an office off the front hall. Amee-nah's mother was already sitting there with a big smile on her face. She motioned for her son to sit next to her. Coach K came in behind the boys. When everyone was seated, Coach began to speak. For Amee-nah's mother's information, he explained how Mawee had asked him to look at Amee-nah's foot to see if anything could be done to straighten it. He told how Mawee had talked Amee-nah into showing his long-hidden foot. He explained what he had learned from his careful examination.

Next he turned and looked directly at Amee-nah. "I'm sorry I wasn't able to tell you more about the surgery. I'm going to have a doctor look at your foot. The doctor will explain every detail of what needs to be done. He will tell exactly how long it will take to heal. He'll answer all your questions."

"Coach K, I'm sorry to interrupt, but I decided I don't want to have an operation," Amee-nah murmured with tears in his eyes. "It will hurt too much."

"But, Amee-nah, when I told you about the pain yesterday it didn't seem to bother you at all," Coach K reminded the tearful boy.

"Coach K, I don't think my son is telling you the real reason for changing his mind. I'm sure it's because of money. He doesn't want you to know it. Last night as soon as I mentioned money everything changed. Amee-nah's smile was gone instantly," the boy's mother explained.

"That's the other reason I wanted both of you to come over today. I wish I would have had this letter yesterday. It just came this morning. As soon as I read it, Amee-nah, I stopped by to see your mother to ask her to come today. From your house I went to your school with the note they gave you. I wanted you both here so I could share this letter with you. I'll read it," Coach K said.

Dear Coach K,

Thank you for telling me about your young friend, Amee-nah, and your suspicion that he has a clubfoot. If you find he needs surgery to correct his condition, please let me know. I will be happy to stop by Zuni and do the procedure to correct the problem. As you know, I was born with a clubfoot. Successful surgery corrected my deformity. I went on to play football, basketball, and baseball in high school. I earned an athletic scholarship to college and was able to go to medical school to become an orthopedic surgeon.

I guess you know all of this. Many people made it possible for me to have my foot surgery. Many people made it possible for me to become a doctor. Now I want to make it possible for this young man to have his operation and be able to walk and run like all of his friends. There will be no charge for my services.

If you find that Amee-nah has a clubfoot, please tell him I'm coming through New Mexico in three weeks on my way to California. I plan some extra days in Zuni. We'll take a look at his foot, make arrangements at the hospital for operating room time, and work out all the details that need to be taken care of. There will be some expenses for the technicians and the hospital.

Friends of mine from our church who are supporters of this mission school want to help by paying the costs of his hospital stay. There will be only one charge for Amee-nah's mother to pay. I would love to have a piece of her beautiful pottery that you described to me.

Please let me know soon if all of this is a go. I'll get busy with all the arrangements. I hope and pray that we can help this boy.

I hope everything is going well for you in your important work at our mission school. See you soon.

Your friend,
Dr. Mike

Amee-nah was stunned. He sat all choked up. He couldn't utter a word. It was unbelievable. Yesterday he was excited to hear Coach K say surgery could make it possible for him to have two normal feet. Soon after, he was determined to give it all up because it would cost more than his mother could afford. Now this letter had come. A doctor from far away in Grand Rapids, Michigan, was coming to make his dream come true for the cost of a piece of pottery. Unreal.

"Coach K, I don't know what to say. I'm sure Amee-nah wants to have the operation. He came home yesterday happier than I have ever seen him. Then came the money problem. He's a good boy. He would go on limping the rest of his life before he would ask me to take out a loan and have to work for years to pay it back. Coach K, I don't know how to thank you. Son, what do you think?" the boy's mother asked. "What do you have to say to Coach K?"

Amee-nah swallowed. He tried to control his feelings. "Coach, thank you. Thank you. Sure, I want the operation," the boy stammered.

"Coach K, please tell Dr. Mike I'll make him a set of three beautiful bowls. They will be originals. Tell him there will be a special piece of pottery for each of his friends. This is a wonderful day for the two of us. And Mawee, what a tremendous friend you are! I know my son is proud to call you his friend. We will be grateful to you and Coach K forever," Amee-nah's mother proclaimed.

"Well, that's it," Coach K laughed. "It's going to happen. I'll notify Dr. Mike right away. As soon as I know more, I'll let everyone know. Amee-nah, my friend, you have a great mom. Take good care of her. I'll see you both again soon."

Coach K stood up, opened the door, and waited outside of the school's front door as everyone said their good-byes and headed for home.

The walk home for Amee-nah and his mother was full of talk about all that had happened. That night they explained everything to Uncle James. He agreed that it all sounded too good to be true. He said it was all meant to be, and he believed nothing happened by accident. Amee-nah's mother felt the same way.

The big news came ten days later. Dr. Mike would arrive in a week. He had already made all the arrangements at Presbyterian Hospital in Albuquerque to do the surgery on Amee-nah's foot. Dr. Mike knew the people at the hospital. First X rays would have to be taken. Next Dr. Mike would consult with everyone involved in the surgery before the actual operation. After the surgery Amee-nah would remain in the hospital for several days. Most likely he would have a cast on his foot and walk with crutches for six or eight weeks. Then the therapy would begin to improve the circulation to his reconstructed toes.

Dr. Mike took time to write to Amee-nah telling him he would have to be tough. He would have to suffer some pain. He would have to make up his mind to take it one day at a time. Dr. Mike said each day would be a little better than the day before, but there would be some discouraging setbacks, too.

"Mom, I'm ready for anything. I'm not going to change my mind. I want this operation more than anything else. I'm ready," Amee-nah told his mother right after he read Dr. Mike's letter.

"Son, I have a vision of you and Mawee running side by side. That wonderful day is coming. I know this deep down in my heart."

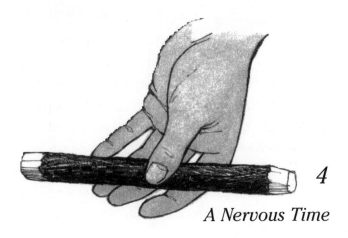

4

A Nervous Time

Amee-nah showed Mawee Dr. Mike's letter.

"Wow! It's really going to happen!" cried Mawee. "And Dr. Mike is coming right while we will be having the stick races. I bet you will miss our big race, but that's okay. Next year you'll probably be stick racing."

"I don't know how long I'll be in the hospital. If I miss the races, it's okay. I just want to get this over with," Amee-nah answered.

The next week was an anxious one for Amee-nah. He didn't see much of Mawee. Mawee was practicing every day for the big stick races.

Coach K stopped by Amee-nah's house two days before Dr. Mike's planned arrival. It was Friday afternoon. He told the boy and his mother that Monday would be the big day. Coach K said he would come over early Monday morning with the school car to drive them to Albuquerque. On Monday afternoon they would arrive at the hospital. By that time the X rays of Amee-nah's foot would be ready for the doctor to read. The next day the doctor would do the operation. Coach K had even arranged a place for Amee-nah's mother to stay while in the city. A family near the hospital had a spare room for her to use free of charge.

Sunday night before his big trip Amee-nah was almost too excited to sleep. Mawee had taken Blinky home with him. The little lamb was already eating hay and grain. He would be well taken care of while Amee-nah was away.

Monday morning the boy was up before daylight. His things were all packed. He had ridden in a car only a few times in his whole life. The car ride would be a thrill. The mission school owned a shiny black 1936 Chevrolet sedan. On Saturday Coach K let Amee-nah sit in it. It was a beauty.

Amee-nah ate his breakfast as the eastern sky was beginning to brighten. His mother had Dr. Mike's pottery all boxed and ready to go along with some more pottery for his friends.

The boy hardly knew what to do with himself while they waited for Coach K to drive up. He was due at 6:30 A.M. At 6:15 Amee-nah looked out the window for at least the twenty-fifth time. He kept checking to see if Coach K might be early. This time the boy broke into a big smile. He jerked open the front door and ran outside. There stood Mawee with a wide grin on his face.

"Hey, Amee-nah, I had to come to see you off. Sure wish I could go along. The school car is neat. Keep your eye on the speedometer. I want to know how fast Coach K drives," Mawee demanded.

"I'm glad you came. How's Blinky?" Amee-nah inquired.

"He's doing great. I can't believe how big he is already. When you come to sheep camp with me, we can let Blinky go back to the flock. He'll make it just fine, thanks to you," Mawee bragged.

"I'm glad you'll be taking care of Blinky. I won't have to worry about him. I only wish his other eye had healed like the good one did," Amee-nah commented wishfully.

"Hey, Amee-nah, I've got something for you to take along. It will remind you that I'm thinking about you," Mawee promised.

Mawee handed Amee-nah a stick about eight inches long. It was about as big around as Amee-nah's finger. It was covered with bark except for a half inch at each end where the bark had been peeled away.

"This is the stick my team used in our big stick race last year. We didn't win, but it was close. This year we'll cross the finish line first. You'll hear all about it when you get back," Mawee said with pride.

Amee-nah had dreamed of running in a stick race someday. As the years passed he gradually gave up the idea. Now because of Mawee, Coach K, and Dr. Mike, his dream just might come true.

The team of four stick racers had to be fast, agile, and able to run for almost twenty-five miles while kicking a stick. A race would take all afternoon. Very seldom would all four team members finish the grueling race.

The racers ran barefoot wearing only a breech-cloth. When they came to the stick, they had to slide their toes under it, scoop it up, and send it flying. Team members worked together to keep the stick moving as fast as possible over the long race course.

All the Zuni people from miles around came to see the exciting contests. Often people would place bets on their favorite team. Most bets were friendly. A few people would bet a lot of money on their team.

During the races, Amee-nah was always off by himself. He had a favorite place on a hillside where he could see the start of the race and still be away from all the people.

"Mawee, thanks a lot. I'll keep your stick with me all the time. I promise you I will start running as soon as my foot heals, and I hope I can make sheep camp this summer," Amee-nah said hopefully.

"Here comes Coach K," Mawee shouted as he spun around to see the shiny black car turn onto Amee-nah's street.

Amee-nah felt a chill from his head to his toes. *This is it,* he thought. *I'm on my way.* He turned toward his door motioning for Mawee to follow him. The boys went in and came out carrying the boxes of pottery. Two worn suitcases were already outside by the front door.

Coach K drove up, parked, and jumped out of the car. "Hi, guys!" he called. "We'll put most of your things in the trunk. Amee-nah, it looks like you're ready. We have a long ride ahead of us. I bet you're pretty excited," Coach K predicted.

Amee-nah's mother came out in time to hear Coach K mention excitement. "Excited isn't the word. This boy was up before the sun. He hasn't sat down or stayed in one place for two minutes," she explained.

"Well, Amee-nah, anyone would be excited on a day like this. You'll do great. Good old Dr. Mike will fix that foot once and for all. Mawee had better train hard. Pretty soon you'll be right on his heels," Coach K teased.

"Maybe I shouldn't have given him my stick. He'll probably start practicing in the hospital hallways." Mawee laughed.

"Don't worry. It will be a long time before I start learning to walk again. Besides, no one can outrun you. They don't call you Mawee for nothing," Amee-nah replied.

After everything was loaded, Amee-nah climbed into the back seat. His mother sat in front. The boy rolled his window down.

"See ya, Mawee. Thanks for the stick. Thanks for taking care of Blinky. Thanks for everything," Amee-nah said with a tremble in his voice.

"Bye now, Amee-nah. I'll come to see you as soon as you get back. Every morning Coach K and I will say a prayer for you," Mawee promised.

Coach K put the car in gear and slowly pulled away. Amee-nah looked out the back window. Mawee was waving away. Amee-nah poked his arm out the side window. He waved until Coach K turned the corner and Mawee was no longer in sight.

Coach K turned onto the main road leading east out of Zuni. Amee-nah's eyes were glued to all the passing sights. Coach K and his mother were talking, but the boy paid no attention to them. His mind was racing with all kinds of thoughts. He was trying to imagine all the things that were going to happen to him in the next few days.

The farthest Amee-nah had ever been from home was Gallup. He had only been there a few times. Not too many miles from Zuni, Coach K turned north on the road to Gallup. In Gallup he turned east on Route 66. Before leaving Gallup Coach K made a stop for gas. While a man was filling the gas tank, Coach K walked next door and bought everyone an ice cream cone.

Route 66 would take them right into Albuquerque. It was so hot in the car that every window was rolled down. The whole trip from Zuni to the big city was about 170 miles. It took all morning to make the drive.

The hospital in Albuquerque was huge. The whole city fascinated Amee-nah. All the people seemed to be in a hurry to get where they were going. All the cars, all the people, all the tall buildings made Amee-nah feel very small. He was just a small boy coming to the big city to have a twisted foot fixed. None of these people had any idea it was such a dramatic time in this Zuni boy's life.

Coach K parked in the hospital parking lot. He led Amee-nah and his mother in through the main entrance. They walked to a large counter. A sign above said, ADMITTING. Coach K gave the lady behind the counter a sheet of paper. The paper had Amee-nah's name, address, reason for his visit, his mother's name, and Dr. Mike's name, all neatly written.

The lady looked at the paper, smiled, and said, "Hello, Amee-nah. We've been expecting you. Your doctor has told us all about you. You must be excited. We're going to do everything we can to help you. Please have a seat while we fill out some papers for you."

"Miss, is there time for us to have lunch in the cafeteria?" Coach K inquired.

"Certainly," the woman replied. "Amee-nah's X rays are scheduled for 2 P.M. There's plenty of time. Just come back when you've finished."

When Amee-nah entered the hospital he felt himself quiver with a mixture of excitement and fear. He clutched the stick Mawee had given him so tightly that his right hand ached. The woman's friendly words put him more at ease.

The cafeteria had lots of delicious food to choose from, but Amee-nah was too full of nervous energy to eat. His stomach was doing flipflops. He was happy when they could finally leave the cafeteria and return to the woman at the counter.

At the admitting counter they were met by a nurse who said Amee-nah could call her Jane. Nurse Jane led everyone to the elevator. The elevator ride terrified the boy. He had never ridden in one. His stomach bounced when the elevator started up. When it jerked to a stop, his stomach sank. He was glad to walk out onto a steady surface.

The children's ward at the end of the hall was a long room with beds sticking out from both walls.

Curtains could be pulled around on metal rods for privacy. Amee-nah looked at the children in this ward. Some looked very sick and were lying in bed without moving. A few were sitting up coloring or reading. Some beds were empty. A few kids stared as Amee-nah limped down the aisle. One boy waved to him.

Nurse Jane stopped near the far end of the ward and cheerfully said, "Here's your bed, Amee-nah. I'll show your mother the playroom while you go for your X rays. There are lots of games, books, and art supplies there. You can use anything you like. Your doctor will be here at about four o'clock to visit with you and your mom. I hope you have a good stay with us. Let me know if there's anything you need."

"Thank you," Amee-nah replied softy.

Amee-nah's mother and Coach K also thanked the nurse. Then Coach K said his good-byes to the boy and his mother. He was due back to work at the mission school the next day. He promised to call the hospital every day to check on Amee-nah's progress.

It was hard for the boy to say good-bye to Coach K. He was learning to admire the man who was doing so much for him. Coach K gave Amee-nah a pat on the back and wished him well. The boy watched as Coach K walked toward the door of the children's ward. At the doorway Coach turned and gave Amee-nah a thumbs up and walked away.

After his visit to the X ray lab and his blood test, Amee-nah returned to his bed. His mother was waiting with a checkerboard all set and ready to play. They passed an hour playing checkers and talking about Mawee, Coach K, and their trip.

A little after four o'clock Amee-nah noticed a man walking into the ward. The man had brown hair with gray sideburns. The man's eyes seemed to be searching the ward for something.

When the man spotted Amee-nah, he broke into a big smile. "Hi, Amee-nah. I'm Dr. Mike. How are you? I'm glad you had a safe trip," the doctor said cheerfully. "This must be your mother. I'm happy to finally meet both of you."

"Hello, Doctor," said Amee-nah's mother as she shook the doctor's hand. "How can I thank you for all you are going to do for my son? I have your pottery with me. Surely that is not nearly enough. My son is so excited. He's been waiting for this day for a long time. Thank you again."

"Listen, I'm so happy to be able to help this young man. Look. You can see I have two good feet. That's because a doctor helped me get rid of my twisted foot when I was a boy. Now let's get to work to help Amee-nah.

"I saw your X rays," he said to Amee-nah. "I have good news. I have seen lots of clubfeet that are much worse than yours. I am sure we can fix it for you. Let's have a closer look, and I'll explain exactly what we'll do to correct the problem."

Amee-nah liked Dr. Mike instantly. He had a deep, friendly voice. His smile was warm and sincere. He was very tall and looked very strong. His hands were large and steady.

Now this man, who only minutes before was a complete stranger, would tell Amee-nah exactly what he would do to the boy's foot the next morning as he lay unconscious on the operating table. Some of the doctor's words would terrify Amee-nah. Words at the end of Dr. Mike's talk would help the boy stay calm and at ease as he prepared to face the most difficult and scary time of his young life.

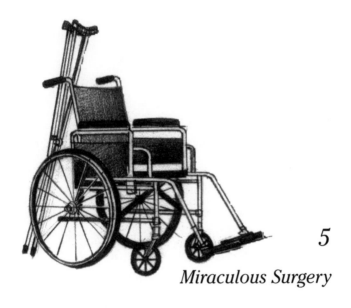

5

Miraculous Surgery

Dr. Mike had Amee-nah sit propped up in his bed. The doctor took the twisted foot in his hands. With his finger tips he probed every inch of the bone structure. When the doctor was satisfied with his investigation he smiled and put Amee-nah's foot back on the bed.

"Amee-nah, I'm sure we can make your foot as good as new. Tomorrow at 7 A.M. we will do your operation. Do not eat anything the rest of today and no breakfast in the morning. I will have lots of help in the operating room. You will be put into a deep sleep. You will feel no pain during surgery. While you're asleep, I'll be able to line up the small bones in your foot. We then will line up your tendons and ligaments to hold your foot straight. When we finish, we'll stitch your foot. A cast will be put on from your toes up over your knee. The cast will hold everything in place, and the healing will begin. You'll have to remain in the hospital for a week or so. Then your cast will be removed so the healing can be checked and the stitches removed. Next, another even tighter cast will be put on your foot and leg. This second cast will have to stay on for eight weeks. After it comes off, you'll need to wear a brace for another six or eight weeks. The hospital in Blackrock will check on you and remove your second cast. They will give you your brace. You will have to use a wheelchair and crutches while the cast and the brace are doing their jobs. You will be told when it's okay to start using your foot. If you follow all these instructions, I think your foot will heal perfectly. You will have some pain through every stage of your recovery. You'll have to be patient and very brave. Well, young man, what do you think?" Dr. Mike asked.

"I'll do anything you say, doctor. I just want to get it over with so I can walk and run without having to limp all the time. I'm ready!" Amee-nah proclaimed with determination in his voice

"Okay then, I'll see you in the morning, bright and early," the doctor commented as he rose to leave. Dr. Mike smiled at Amee-nah and his mother as he turned and walked away.

Amee-nah sat on the edge of his bed in deep thought. He started adding up the weeks in his mind. A week in the hospital, eight weeks in a cast, at least six weeks in a brace meant summer would be half over before he could take his first steps. What about school? What about sheep camp? What about Blinky? This was way more time than he had thought it would take. Before, he had guessed the surgery and a short healing time would do it. Now he was faced with over three months of recovery time, maybe longer.

"Son, I can guess what you're thinking. Even I didn't think it would take so long for your foot to heal. We know Dr. Mike knows what's best. I'm going to help you through all of this."

"Mom, I don't care how long it takes. I've had this twisted foot for ten years. Now I'm going to do everything Dr. Mike says. All I want to do is get rid of my crooked foot," Amee-nah declared.

Amee-nah didn't sleep very well in this strange place. Besides, all he could think about was his operation. When he finally went to sleep, one of the other kids had a nightmare and began screaming loudly. A nurse came running in to comfort the frightened child.

When morning finally came, Nurse Jane came in to take Amee-nah's pulse and his blood pressure. A few minutes later the boy's mother walked in. She told him how nice the family was where she had spent the night. They were happy to have her stay as long as she wanted.

On Nurse Jane's second trip into the ward she cheerfully called, "Amee-nah, let's go. Everything is ready." The nurse carefully bathed the boy's twisted foot and ankle with special cleansing chemicals.

The boys heart began to beat faster and faster. He felt a little shaky as the nurse wheeled him down the hall on a narrow bed with wheels to the operating room. At the door the boy's mother gave him a hug and said she would be waiting nearby and would see him soon. Amee-nah handed Mawee's stick to her. As he rolled into the bright white room, he never felt more alone in his life.

"Hop up on this table," Nurse Jane instructed. "Dr. Mike will be here in a few minutes."

Almost like a robot, Amee-nah lifted himself onto the table covered with a bright white sheet. He straightened his clumsy hospital gown. He barely had a chance to look around before Dr. Mike was standing at his side.

"Well Amee-nah, you look great. I imagine you're a little scared. I want you to know that everyone here is going to make sure you do fine. Thousands of people have surgery. When you wake up, it will be all over. Your body will take over and heal itself. The human body is a miraculous thing. Yours is strong and healthy. Just relax now, and we'll do the rest."

Before he knew it, someone placed something over his nose and mouth, and Amee-nah fell into a deep sleep. He dreamed and dreamed. All of his dreams ran together one after another. He only remembered one thing from all his dreaming. It was the same clapping sound he had heard in other dreams.

Amee-nah's surgery was finished. He was rolled into the recovery room on his operating table and lifted onto a bed. As he lay there, he thought he heard voices. His eyes blinked open. He seemed to be spinning around and around. He closed his eyes. He felt very weak and sleepy. He could hear the voices again. Finally someone called his name.

"Amee-nah, Amee-nah, are you awake? I'm Nurse Jane. Your mom is right here next to me. Your surgery is over. Your foot is as straight as can be. The cast is in place. You're going to be as good as new."

Amee-nah fought to focus his eyes. His throat was as dry as a desert. He had no feeling in his body. He was still groggy from his deep sleep.

When the boy finally gained control of his eyes, he saw his mother standing over him. Tears were coming down her cheeks. She managed a smile and squeezed her son's hand.

"Son, I'm here. You are doing fine. I'm proud of you. Dr. Mike says the surgery was easier than he thought it would be. He said your foot should heal perfectly. He's coming to see you later today. You have to stay here a little longer, then we can go back to the ward."

The boy was happy to hear his mother's voice. He was so woozy he wouldn't remember a word she said.

That afternoon Amee-nah was feeling much better. He was still a little shaky. He drank lots of orange juice. Nurse Jane gave him pain pills to control the pain that had already started. The pills made him sleepy.

Just before supper Dr. Mike came in and had a long visit with the boy and his mother. Again he told Amee-nah all about the details of his recovery. He warned him to be very careful and to follow the directions of the people at the clinic in Zuni. Dr. Mike said he would see him once more in the morning and then have to leave for California.

Amee-nah's hospital stay seemed to drag on slowly. Coach K called and heard the good news about the successful surgery. The boy's mother came every day. They read books and played games by the hour.

The cast felt heavy. The pain in Amee-nah's foot would often begin to throb and burn. The next pain pill would ease the pain each time. By the end of the week Amee-nah's appetite was back. He was getting restless to leave for home. On Saturday his mother came in with the exciting news.

"Son, Nurse Jane says your cast comes off Tuesday morning. They will take your stitches out and put on a new cast. Coach K will be here before noon to take us home."

Amee-nah broke into a big smile. *Three more days and I head for home. I can't wait,* Amee-nah thought.

When that long-awaited Tuesday morning came, Amee-nah watched excitedly as his cast was cut

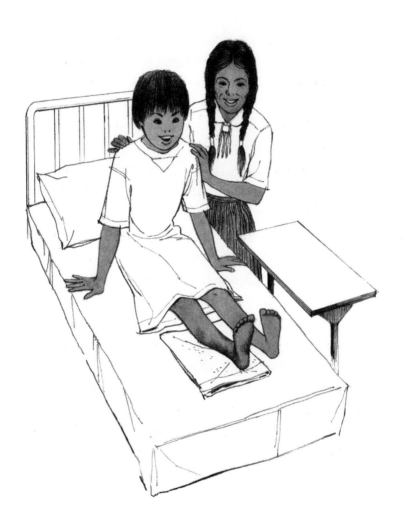

away. He had his very first look at his new foot. He could hardly believe his eyes. The twisted foot was straight. But the incision looked scary, and his foot was swollen. A lot more healing would be needed. Now he would begin living for the day this second cast could be removed.

Coach K came in time to wheel Amee-nah out to the car in his wheelchair. He was giving the boy all the latest news from back home. It was quite a job to get Amee-nah into the back seat. He rested his cast across the whole seat. His crutches were laid on the floor. Coach K tied the wheelchair on the cartop carrier. Amee-nah would need both crutches and wheelchair to get around for the next two months. He would be sure to keep his weight off his healing foot no matter what.

On the drive home Coach K said Mawee was going to be waiting for Amee-nah. Coach had to promise not to tell the outcome of the stick races. Mawee wanted to do that himself.

Another stop was made in Gallup for gas and ice cream. The closer Amee-nah came to home the more excited he became. His eyes soaked in all the familiar scenery. His favorite mesa, Towayalane, signaled the end of the journey was near. The giant mountain rose from the valley just southeast of Zuni.

Coach K drove into the Zuni pueblo just as schools were dismissing. As he turned onto Amee-nah's street, Mawee sprinted around the corner. He ran next to the slowly moving car waving wildly.

Coach K eased the car to a stop in front of Amee-nah's house. Mawee jerked the back door open.

"Wow, look at you! Where'd you get that monster?" cried Mawee.

"Hi, Mawee! Boy, am I glad to see you! How you doing?" Amee-nah yelled. "It's great to be back. Have I got a lot to tell you. How's Blinky?"

"He's behind your house in the outside pen. He's doing great," Mawee said.

This was one exciting day. All of Amee-nah's aunts and uncles came to see him. Everyone wanted to hear the whole story. The boy and his mother told it over and over again. All the kids took turns trying Amee-nah's crutches and wheelchair.

Amee-nah had very little time to spend with Mawee or Blinky.

Amee-nah was glad when everyone finally went home. He was exhausted. His leg had begun to throb in his cast. He had forgotten to take his pain pill.

That night Amee-nah slept better than he had since he left over a week ago. The next day he spent practicing with his wheelchair. He worked so hard at it that his arms ached. He had blisters on his hands from working so hard. By the next Monday he would be ready to head back to school.

When Mawee came over the next day, Amee-nah heard about the stick races. Mawee's team came in second again. They were ahead for most of the race. The best team in the whole village defeated them in the last hundred yards. It was a heartbreaking loss. The winning team was older and more experienced. Even so, Mawee said his team would have won except for some bad breaks early in the race when the stick seemed to land in very bad places after many of the best kicks.

Mawee was sorry to hear how long Amee-nah had to be in a cast. "Amee-nah, you and Blinky can still make the last month of sheep camp. We can still have fun," Mawee jabbered. "We have to get Blinky back in the flock before he gets too old. He's ready."

Monday was a big day. Amee-nah headed back to school. He wheeled himself all the way to school. He had to go through the delivery door where there were no steps. For a while all the kids stared at his cast and his wheelchair, but they soon became used to them.

Amee-nah was able to use his crutches more and more every day. In a week he could use them amazingly well. He was also getting use to the dull pain in his foot and ankle. His leg began to itch like crazy.

Day in and day out Amee-nah rolled himself to school and back home in the afternoon. His arms were getting stronger and stronger. He no longer took pain pills.

The day school dismissed for the summer Amee-nah would go to the clinic in Zuni where his cast would be removed and a brace attached to his lower leg, ankle, and foot.

When that day came, Amee-nah would finally have a long look at his new foot. He didn't realize how much pain was in store for him when the protective cast was cut away. He had no idea that he would have to endure shear agony before the foot could be used normally and all the pain would be gone.

6

Minute-by-Minute Excitement

Every student in every school is excited on the last day of school before summer vacation. The most excited student in all of Zuni had to be Amee-nah. Not only would vacation begin, but right after school that day he would have his cast removed. The long eight weeks would be over. Finally the boy would have a good look at his new foot.

When the final bell rang, Amee-nah was on his crutches and out the delivery door. He broke into a big grin when he saw Mawee waiting next to his wheelchair. With Amee-nah in the chair Mawee grabbed the handles and shoved his friend out onto the street.

"Hang on! Here we go!" shouted Mawee.

"Yahoo!" cried Amee-nah.

What a sight they were heading full speed down the street to the clinic. Coach K and Amee-nah's mother were already there waiting for the boys' arrival.

The people at the clinic went right to work on the heavy cast. Bit by bit they carefully cut it away. Amee-nah's leg was wrinkled and faded in color. It was all shriveled and weak looking. The boy stared at his leg, especially the long cut Dr. Mike had made during surgery.

"Yuk!" Amee-nah blurted. "It looks scary. Boy, it itches like mad."

"Wow! What a scar!" Mawee proclaimed. "Does it hurt?"

"It doesn't hurt much, but the itching is unbeliev-able." Amee-nah replied.

The nurse gently rubbed a salve on the boy's leg and foot. It was just what he needed to help relieve the itching. He felt much better when she had finished.

Next came the brace. Amee-nah had to lie perfectly still while the brace was put in place. The brace started just below the boy's knee and fit next to both sides of his leg. The lower end of the brace was attached to both sides of a shoe-boot.

The nurse told Amee-nah that he was to avoid putting any weight on his foot for at least four weeks. After four weeks his foot would be examined again. At that time they would decide if he could start putting his foot down or not.

Amee-nah's leg felt amazingly light without the bulky cast. Not long after the brace was secured, the boy's leg began to ache. The pain increased by the minute. His leg was letting him know how tender and weak it was.

The boy was told his leg would ache for several days. He was given some pills to help dull the pain. All the while Amee-nah lay on the table in the clinic, Mawee stood by unable to take his eyes off his friend's leg and foot.

"I can't believe it. It's fantastic. Dr. Mike made your foot perfectly straight. It's a miracle," Mawee stated enthusiastically.

"I can't believe it myself. When I saw my foot after my operation, I didn't even think it was mine. Now I can't wait to start walking on it," Amee-nah said.

Mawee pushed Amee-nah home where the next stage of healing would begin. Mawee said so long to his friend. Mawee would be off to sheep camp the next morning. He promised to visit Amee-nah every time he came back into the pueblo.

During the next four weeks Coach K checked on him often. Several letters came from Dr. Mike. Amee-nah's pain decreased a little each day. The boy was glad the cast was gone. He could even move his foot a little. He made sure not to put any weight on his foot.

Amee-nah had lots of time to spend with Blinky. The lamb had grown fast and was doing well with its one good eye.

Finally, at the end of the four weeks, the hospital people in Blackrock told him he could start putting a little weight at a time on his foot. They explained that the pain would tell him if he was putting too much weight down too soon. Too much pain meant too much weight. He was told to take it slow and easy.

All night Amee-nah thought, *Here I go. I'm going to be walking in no time.*

The boy stood for the first time without his cast. His crutches allowed him to put his new foot down lightly. What a strange feeling it was. At first there was little feeling in his foot or leg.

Then it hit. A sharp pain shot from his foot to his ankle. Instantly Amee-nah lifted his foot off the floor. In a few moments the pain diminished. Then and there the boy realized it was not going to be so easy after all.

It wasn't easy. Day by day Amee-nah tested his new foot. Day by day he was able to use his foot a little more. The boy lived with the pain. He was careful to use his foot only a little more at a time to control the pain. His leg muscles which hadn't been used for weeks began to ache as they took on more and more weight. He was glad to be able to move his toes more and more.

"Son, you are doing so well. I'm proud of you. You have done everything Dr. Mike and the hospital people have asked you to do," Amee-nah's mother told him.

"Mom, next week it's all over. They're going to take the brace off for good. I can already put most of my weight down. It hardly hurts. I can't wait. I thought this time would never come," the boy told his mother.

"Son, your dream is coming true," the proud mother stated.

Both the boy and his mother were happy that the long ordeal was almost over. When the brace came off, Amee-nah would have to use his crutches only as long as he needed them. One day soon he would walk completely on his own, no cast, no brace, no crutches, and no limp. What a day that would be!

Amee-nah had no way of knowing about the big surprise that awaited him at the hospital in Blackrock on this final visit. The hospital was buzzing with activity. The back room would be the scene of the big surprise.

As usual Amee-nah was asked to come into an examination room. The boy stretched out on the examination table. The nurse carefully removed the boot and brace. She told Amee-nah that he had been a wonderful patient. She explained that his crutches would still be needed until he could walk without great pain.

With the brace off, Amee-nah smiled and thanked the nurse for all her help. He promised to use his crutches until his foot could take his full weight. When he turned to leave, he tested his new foot for the first time without a cast or a brace. With a regular shoe his foot felt very strange. His excitement was so great that he had to force himself to concentrate on the simple task of walking. Using his new foot, Amee-nah slowly moved toward the door.

"Oh! Amee-nah, I almost forgot. You have to come with me to have your picture taken for our records," the nurse explained. "Please follow me."

The nurse opened the door to the back room so Amee-nah could walk in. As the boy entered the room, a loud roar went up.

"Surprise!"

Amee-nah was shocked. There stood Coach K, Mawee, Amee-nah's mother, his Uncle James, and all the rest of his uncles, aunts, and cousins. A huge cake sat on a table. Balloons and crepe paper hung from the light fixtures.

What a party it was! Everyone gave Amee-nah a hug and told him how proud of him they were. They all laughed at the decoration on the frosting. It was the outline of a foot. Everyone enjoyed the delicious cake and pink punch.

Within a week Amee-nah was putting almost all of his weight on his new foot. Now the pain was hardly noticeable. Several times he tried walking short distances without crutches. At first the boy felt unsure of himself.

Soon Amee-nah was walking around his house with no crutches. He experienced some pain in his foot and even in his leg. Gradually even this pain began to disappear. The boy was determined to strengthen his foot and walked a little farther each day. His limp was gone.

Three weeks after the brace came off, Amee-nah was walking over a mile a day. His only pain was the aching in his leg muscles. Those muscles hadn't been used for over three months. They were adjusting to their new work.

Amee-nah's mother would often watch her son walk down the street. She was full of joy to see her son doing so well. She often talked to Amee-nah about the miracle Dr. Mike had done. She talked about what wonderful friends Mawee and Coach K were.

"Mom, Mawee saw me yesterday. He wants me to visit sheep camp. Do you think I should?" Amee-nah asked.

The boy almost hoped his mother would say he shouldn't. He wasn't sure he wanted to. It meant he would have to say good-bye to Blinky. Amee-nah had come to love the little lamb while he helped it recover from its injuries.

"Sure, you should go. You've earned a special adventure. You'll have a great time. It will be good for Blinky to return to the flock before winter. He needs to live a normal life."

That was it. His mother was right. It would be selfish to keep Blinky away from the flock. He had to do what was best for the lamb. Besides, he had promised Mawee he would make sheep camp before summer ended. Now he would keep that promise.

It was a bright sunny morning when Mawee and his father drove up in their old Ford pickup truck. Amee-nah's things were all packed. Mawee's dad lifted Blinky into the back of the pickup. The two boys piled in with the lamb and Amee-nah's bag. Amee-nah's mother handed him a sack of hard candy and waved as the truck pulled away.

"Wow! Can you believe it? We're on our way. I thought this day would never come," shouted Mawee over the noise of the truck.

"I'm glad you still want me to come with you. My foot is ready. Maybe I can even do a little running," hollered Amee-nah as the truck rumbled on.

Sheep camp was seven miles from Zuni. Mawee's father had built the camp years ago. He built the walls with flat sandstone slabs. A claylike mortar held the rocks together. A wooden roof made a nice cozy room. Bunks were built along each wall. Cooking was done outside over an open fire.

After settling in, Mawee took Amee-nah on a tour of the area. Blinky was tied to a small cedar tree while Mawee showed Amee-nah the flock of sheep. He pointed to all the places that the sheep could graze. Amee-nah was surprised to see how far the sheep could roam. He explained the work they would do each day. Their long runs would allow them to check on the safety of all the sheep scattered over the hillsides.

While school was out, Zuni boys cared for the sheep. This gave their fathers time to spend raising corn, other vegetables, and feed for the sheep. One man would be in charge of several sheep camps. Mawee was checked on by old Joshua. The old shepherd made sure all was well with Mawee and his sheep.

Amee-nah found out two other boys, John and Paul, lived with Mawee. They slept in two of the bunks. The fourth bunk would be Amee-nah's. John and Paul were brothers. Mawee said they were great stick racers. He said they were on the team that had beaten his team the spring before.

"John and Paul are good guys," Mawee explained. "They're always reminding me about their big run. I just tell 'em, wait till next year."

The first morning at sheep camp the boys were up at daybreak. They talked about Amee-nah's visit and his amazing operation. John and Paul had to see the scar on Amee-nah's foot. They asked lots of questions about every detail of the boy's ordeal.

After breakfast, the boys prepared to head out and check the sheep. Amee-nah took Blinky along on a leash. The lamb was very alert and excited. It seemed to know something big was going to happen. Blinky's nose was taking in all the familiar smells. Suddenly the lamb began bleating loudly. Nearby sheep answered.

"Isn't this great?" Mawee whispered. "Blinky knows he's going home. I wonder if the flock has a cake baked for him." Mawee laughed.

"This is a big day for Blinky. I kind of hate to see him leave. I know it's best. I hope he makes it okay," Amee-nah said hopefully.

The two boys led Blinky into the flock. The lamb was bleating softly and sniffing the air about him. Mawee stopped. He watched Amee-nah walk a little farther into the flock and stop. The boy knelt down next to the excited lamb. He stroked its woolly neck and back.

"Here we are, Blinky. You're back home. I'm glad you made it. I'll be keeping an eye on you. You're big enough that no ravens will dare come near you now. Good-bye, Blinky," Amee-nah whispered.

The boy slipped the leash from the lamb's neck. Without hesitation Blinky bounded off into the flock. Amee-nah watched for a few seconds before he stood and walked back to Mawee.

"Boy, isn't it great! Your foot is all healed and now Blinky is back with the flock. What a summer this has been!" Mawee declared.

Amee-nah knew his friend was exactly right. This summer would never be forgotten. His operation was best of all. Losing Blinky wasn't that great, but it still made Amee-nah feel good to know Blinky was back to normal.

This special summer wasn't over yet. Amee-nah would gradually get used to sheep camp. He would even begin to run short distances. He was able to ignore the minor aches and pains in his muscles. If the boys thought the summer had been unforgettable so far, they would be sure of it before long.

7

Race against Time

Morning after morning the four boys were up bright and early. Cool morning air felt great, but it never took the sun long to heat the air. Morning was Amee-nah's favorite time. Spring water from a large barrel filled a wash basin. The boy cupped water in his hands and splashed it on his face to wake himself.

The four boys talked about the sheep, about school, about summer coming to an end, and many other things. John and Paul told the story of a bobcat attack that happened a month ago. The cat had killed a lamb and a ewe. They said they ended up with a lamb without a mother and a ewe without her lamb.

Paul told how the Zuni shepherd, Joshua, was able to fool the ewe who had lost her lamb. He had a clever way to get the mother to accept the orphaned lamb as her own. Normally a mother sheep would never have anything to do with a strange lamb. The ewe would absolutely refuse to adopt the poor motherless lamb.

"Old Joshua fooled that ewe, but good," Paul bragged. "He took the hide from the dead lamb and cleaned it up with his knife. Then he took the dead lamb's hide and tied it around the orphaned lamb. He said the mother ewe knew her own baby by its smell. With her dead lamb's hide wrapped around the orphan, the mother would be fooled. She would smell her own lamb's hide. She would let the little lamb nurse because she would think it was her own. Believe it or not, it worked. I couldn't believe it. The ewe took the disguised lamb first thing. One day the hide came off and it made no difference. That ewe and lamb are still together. Old Joshua knows all the tricks."

"It's fun to sit and listen to Joshua tell about all the wild adventures he's had. He could write a book," John added.

That very night the old shepherd visited the four boys. He sat with them at the campfire telling tales. Amee-nah loved every minute of his stories. The boys begged the shepherd to tell them the legend of the great flood that hit Zuni in ancient times.

As he always did, the old man thought for a few minutes. Finally he smiled and said all right. Joshua looked out over the land and pointed east toward the great mesa, Towayalane, that rose above the valley like a great wall. He told the boys to look at the sacred tablelike mountain.

Old Joshua told of the great rains that came to the valley. Never had it rained so long and so hard. Day after day the rains continued. Soon all the fields were covered by water. As the waters rose, all the people fled to the top of Towayalane to save themselves.

To the horror of all the people the water continued to rise. Everyone feared that the menacing water would swallow them alive. They feared there would be no Zuni people left on earth.

As the angry waters lapped around the feet of the terrified people, everyone believed the end was near. Mothers and fathers hugged their children. Families and friends spoke their final farewell. All they could do was huddle together and helplessly wait for the end to come.

Strangely, on the edge of the frantic crowd a boy and a girl stood calmly hand in hand. They were the son and daughter of a Zuni spiritual leader. Fearlessly the brave brother and sister began walking into the treacherous waters. The Zuni people watched in absolute horror as the small boy and girl disappeared into the depths of the flood never to be seen again.

Joshua gestured with his hands as he explained that as soon as the children were lost in the flood, the water began to retreat. The surprised people began to shout their thanksgiving for being spared a horrible death. Soon they could walk all the way to the edge of the great mesa. In time all the water would disappear. The people believed the sacrifice of the two children saved the Zuni people.

"Now boys," said old Joshua, "two tall columns of rock stand next to the great mesa. The people believe the two rocky towers represent the two brave children who gave their lives to conquer the mighty flood and save the Zuni people."

Oh, the boys had heard this legend before, but no one told it better than this elder Zuni shepherd. Amee-nah would look forward to every visit from Joshua. The young boy was learning to love and respect the old shepherd.

Every day Mawee and Amee-nah traveled the rough slopes checking the sheep. The animals were spread out over great distances. The plants they grazed on were scarce. The sheep kept moving in search of a food source. Small cedars and pines often hid them from view.

Amee-nah spotted Blinky every once in a while. The lamb was doing well. Blinky would even come up to Amee-nah and let him pet him. The boy loved these visits with the lamb.

Mawee ran long distances, always alert for any trouble or danger to the flock. Amee-nah began running a little more each day. At first his legs ached badly. Little by little he ran greater and greater distances. Gradually he started losing weight. Before his operation he was overweight from lack of exercise. Some of the boys at his school had teased him about being fat. When he returned to school this year, they wouldn't even recognize him.

The summer days passed quickly. Soon the boys would head home and back to school. With just one week left, Amee-nah was running over two miles a day. He still had trouble breathing and couldn't run very fast. His lungs and heart must slowly adjust to the new demands for oxygen. When he became breathless, he would slow down to an easy jog. As the time to return to school came, Amee-nah was nervous. What would the kids think when they saw him walking without a limp?

Would they stare at him? Would they tease him? Some nights Amee-nah could hardly get to sleep.

This afternoon was one of the hottest of the whole summer. Sweat was pouring from Amee-nah's body as he jogged through the sparse cedar trees. He had just made a stop to observe a group of sheep when he thought he heard someone screaming. Quickly he turned his ear toward the sound.

"Mawee, it's Mawee!" Amee-nah cried aloud. "Something's wrong!"

He spun around and ran in the direction of the sound. He heard Mawee scream again. Mawee was calling Amee-nah's name again and again. *What can be wrong?* the boy wondered. *Is Mawee hurt? Have the sheep been attacked?* Frantically Amee-nah sprinted at full speed.

When Amee-nah was close enough, he heard Mawee shriek, "It's Joshua! Hurry! Please, hurry!"

Amee-nah broke through the final clump of trees and came to an abrupt stop. There on the ground lay old Joshua. Mawee was kneeling next to him.

The old shepherd was holding his arms over his upper body and moaning softly.

"Amee-nah! Joshua's in bad shape! I don't know what's wrong! It might be a heart attack! We can't let him die! You stay here! I'm going for help! I'll be back as soon as possible!" Mawee promised.

With that, Mawee raced off toward the nearest road. He was sprinting through trees at top speed, jumping rocks and roots, on a direct line to the road three miles away. Mawee had never run faster. He knew he was in a race to save the fallen shepherd's life.

Amee-nah had yanked his shirt off and folded it into a pillow for Joshua's head. He rubbed the old man's forehead. The shepherd moaned and mumbled something that Amee-nah could not understand.

"Joshua, Mawee has gone for help. He'll be back soon. You're going to be okay. I know you're going to be okay," Amee-nah sobbed.

The boy trembled with fright. He felt helpless. *How could this be happening? Would Mawee find help in time? Would he have to run all the way to*

Zuni? That was at least eight miles. These thoughts caused Amee-nah to shake all over.

"Joshua, are you okay? Are you in pain?"

Amee-nah's questions went unanswered. The shepherd continued to groan. His eyes were rolling. He shivered and fought for every breath.

Amee-nah continued to talk to the fallen man. The minutes seemed like hours. *Would help ever come? Where was Mawee now? Would Joshua die right here?* The boy's horrible thoughts caused him to shudder.

Suddenly, Amee-nah heard someone call his name. Amee-nah shouted back, "Over here! We're over here!"

In seconds John was standing next to Amee-nah and the fallen shepherd. He held three blankets under his arm.

"Mawee told me what happened! I grabbed these three blankets from camp! We have to keep Joshua warm! We have to make him comfortable! Help me!" John demanded.

The boys placed one folded blanket over the ground they had leveled. They gently moved the frail man onto the blanket. They covered him with the other two blankets.

"Where did you see Mawee? How close is he to the road? Do you think he can make it?" Amee-nah whispered.

"That kid can run. He almost beat us single-handed in our last stick race. If anybody can make it, it's Mawee," John assured Amee-nah. "He'll make it. You'll see."

Mawee flew like the wind. He kept telling himself to go faster and faster. He prayed he could make it in time. Several times he stumbled and almost fell. *I can't fall,* he thought. *A fall might mean I won't make it in time.* He knew every second counted.

Mawee's adrenaline was surging through his bloodstream. He felt his power build as he neared the road. Now the road was in sight only a half mile away.

He had just caught sight of the road when suddenly a pickup truck rounded a curve headed for Zuni. The race was on. Mawee realized the truck would pass the spot where he would reach the road. If the truck went by that spot before he could make it there, he would have to run for miles to find another vehicle.

Mawee desperately increased his speed. He saw it was going to be close. The truck was closing in on the spot.

At the last instant Mawee knew he would be just a few seconds too late. He began screaming at the driver at the top of his lungs. It was useless. Mawee had to think fast. The boy quickly scooped up a baseball-sized rock. With a mighty throw he sent the rock flying toward the passing truck. The rock barely cleared the tailgate. It slammed into the bed of the truck, took a big bounce, and struck the rear window behind the driver's head.

The startled driver slammed on the brakes. He stared at his cracked window. The man jumped out by his truck and ran back to see who was guilty of pulling this stupid stunt.

"Help us!" Mawee bellowed. "We need your help!"

"What's going on?" the man hollered at the same time. "What are you doing? You could have killed me."

The angry driver ran toward Mawee to grab him. The boy held his ground gasping for every breath.

"I'm sorry, mister!" Mawee blurted. "Joshua, our shepherd, is dying! We found him on the ground! We need to get him to a doctor! Please help us!"

"Where is he? Quick, hop in my truck! Show me where to go!" the man ordered.

Mawee and the stranger jumped into the cab of the old truck.

"He's up there, near the top," cried Mawee as he pointed southwest from the truck.

The driver made a sharp right turn and started driving cross country, dodging trees and rocks. The truck felt like it would fall apart. Mawee had to hold his hands against the roof or his head would be smashed as he bounced up off the seat.

The driver drove on and on. They were getting close when they were finally stopped by fallen trees and huge rocks. Mawee led the man in a dash to the scene of the emergency.

"Mawee!" cried John. "Boy, are we glad to see you. Old Joshua's doing a little better. He has even

talked a little bit. He says his left arm is numb and his chest aches. We have to get him out of here."

The aged shepherd weighed only one hundred twenty pounds. The man and John lifted him carefully and carried him to the truck. They placed two blankets on the bed of the truck. The other blanket covered the ailing shepherd.

Mawee and Amee-nah jumped in with Joshua. The two boys sat on each side of the shepherd to keep him from rolling off the blankets. With John next to him in the cab, the driver headed the truck back toward the road. The truck crept along to protect Joshua from the bouncing. It was still a very rough ride.

When they passed near the sheep camp, John jumped from the truck. He made a frantic dash to the camp, grabbed two mattresses, and raced back to meet the slowly moving truck.

The driver came to a stop just long enough for the boys to put the mattresses under Joshua. All three blankets were wrapped around the old shepherd. Now the driver could go a little faster.

The straw-filled mattresses would protect the ailing man.

It seemed to take forever to reach the main road. The boys kept telling Joshua he was going to make it. The boys smiled at each other as the driver pulled up onto the road to Zuni. The driver stomped on the accelerator, and the truck roared down the road in a cloud of dust.

Joshua was checked at the clinic in Zuni and then sent by ambulance to Gallup. The three boys could finally breathe a sigh of relief. They began to tremble after it had all ended. The driver, who was a member of a nearby tribe, told the boys they had done a great job. He told Mawee he was glad the rock hit the target. He said the crack in his window would be a reminder of the dramatic rescue.

When the driver left, the boys knew all they could do now was wait. The boys hoped they had not been too late. Only time would tell if the beloved shepherd would ever return to Zuni.

8

Stunned by Tragedy

The good news came the day Mawee and Amee-
nah arrived home from sheep camp. Old Joshua
had left the intensive care unit of the hospital. He
had suffered some heart damage during his attack
but would recover. He would have to take heart
medicine every day and would have regular check-
ups. His days as a shepherd were over.

When Joshua returned to the pueblo, his young
friends would be there to welcome him. They
would visit him often. The shepherd would still be

able to share many more stories with the three boys who had saved his life.

The kids at Amee-nah's school were amazed when they saw the new Amee-nah. He had lost weight. He walked without a limp. He was able to go to regular physical education classes in the gym. He was truly a new person. One way Amee-nah hadn't changed. He was still very quiet and kept to himself.

Almost every day after school, Mawee and Amee-nah took off for the roads that led into the hills. They kicked a stick mile after mile. At first Amee-nah felt awkward and clumsy. He had a hard time getting the stick on his toes just right so he could send it flying. But the more he practiced the better he could do it. Timing was everything. Running at full speed the kicker had to stop without getting too far over the stick. Stopping too soon also wasted time.

Mawee was a great kicker. He could come up to the stick, hardly stop at all, and in one beautiful motion lift the stick and send it flying. Again and again Amee-nah tried to copy Mawee. Once in a while he came close to making a perfect kick. More often he messed up and wasted time recovering.

When Mawee couldn't practice, Amee-nah went out on his own. Soon everywhere he went he was seen kicking a stick. When the weather was good, he slipped off his shoe and kicked his stick to and from school. Sometimes he would go for long runs to strengthen his legs and build up his heart and lung power. In two or three years he hoped to be on a team of stick racers.

It was a very wild winter for weather. There were dust storms, icy winds, freezing rain, and even snow. The snow didn't last very long, but it was exciting. All the children romped through the snow, had snowball fights, and slid down the hillsides on pieces of cardboard.

The weather cut down on Amee-nah's running time, but he was out in some of the bad weather anyway. The boy was glad when a sudden change came. One afternoon in late January the temperature reached seventy-two degrees.

That warm afternoon Mawee and Amee-nah were taking a long run. At the end of their run Mawee told Amee-nah that regular practice for stick racing would begin soon. Mawee said he would be running farther and farther each day. Soon he would be running the course of the whole stick race. In one week the other three runners would join Mawee for practice times.

"When your team comes, I'll just run on my own," Amee-nah told his friend.

"Hey, you can run with us. The guys won't care," Mawee said.

"That's okay. I think it's better for you guys to be together. I'd just hold you back," Amee-nah stated.

"Amee-nah, if you change your mind, you're always welcome. No matter what, this is my team's year to win!" Mawee declared.

Day by day the winter passed. Most days were great for running. Amee-nah was getting stronger and stronger. As March drew closer the stick races were scheduled. The finals would be run at the end of April. With each passing day Amee-nah saw less and less of his good friend. Mawee and his team practiced every chance they had.

Ten days before the big race Mawee and Amee-nah paid a visit to old Joshua. The shepherd was his old self again. Like he did on every visit by the boys, the oldtimer thanked the boys for saving his life. He gave the same speech every time.

"You know, if it wasn't for you boys, I wouldn't be here now. Every time the sun rises I know I have another day on this good earth. I give thanks for you boys and thanks for each new day I have to live."

Amee-nah figured he had heard those same words twenty times. Each time old Joshua spoke those words as though he had just thought of them. The boys knew the old shepherd meant every word of it.

When they left Joshua, Mawee said, "Four more days of practice and my team will be ready for the big race. We'll do nothing but rest the last four days before the race. Fasting will purify our bodies. All four days we'll eat nothing but paper bread. We'll be ready when the big day comes."

Amee-nah wondered if paper bread really did any good. It was just a paper-thin bread made from cornmeal. It surely couldn't satisfy a hungry appetite.

Amee-nah could tell Mawee wanted to win the race more than anything. Mawee's team nearly had won the year before, but the other team was much older and more experienced.

"Hey, Amee-nah, how about practicing with me after school tomorrow. The rest of my team can't practice until after supper. Want to?" Mawee asked.

"Sure. I'll meet you right after school," Amee-nah replied.

With all his practice, Amee-nah was getting pretty good with the stick. To be able to practice with his best friend before such a big race would be a thrill for the boy who dreamed of being in a stick race himself someday.

The next afternoon Amee-nah left school and headed for the place where he had agreed to meet Mawee. A strong wind had come up. Dust filled the air. It was muggy. This almost always meant a storm was coming. Amee-nah hoped Mawee would still want to practice.

Amee-nah met Mawee and found out his friend was glad the wind was blowing so hard. Mawee wanted to practice against the wind. If a wind came up during a race, he would know just what to expect. In a strong wind the racers would kick the stick at an angle to keep it low. This way the wind would not slow it down so much. If the wind was behind them they would send the stick higher so the wind could carry it farther.

The two boys left the pueblo on a narrow dirt road. The wind was blowing into their faces. Mawee showed Amee-nah how to keep the stick low and out of the wind.

The boys were moving surprisingly well in these tough conditions. Mile after mile they kicked the stick. They were following the same course the championship race would follow.

Amee-nah made some great kicks. All his hours of practice had improved his skills greatly. Mawee was impressed with how fast Amee-nah had learned to send the stick flying. He kept giving Amee-nah a thumbs up on every good kick. Amee-nah was having a great time. Not only were his kicks better but his running was improving as well.

After four miles of a grueling run, the boys turned and headed back. Darkening clouds and distant thunder signaled an approaching storm. The wind had become much cooler. The wind at their backs helped the boys speed up. The stick sailed much farther in the twenty-mile-an-hour wind.

The fast-moving storm was rapidly closing in on the racing boys. Mawee finally picked up the stick. The race to beat the storm began.

With every passing minute the thunder became louder and louder. Bolts of lightning shot out of the low-hanging clouds. Huge raindrops began to pelt the boys. Gradually the cold drops of rain increased until the water was coming down in torrents.

Amee-nah was doing his best to keep up with Mawee but gradually fell back. The road was getting slick and treacherous. The boys stuck to the center of the road. The tire ruts were now small streams of water and mud.

A mile from the pueblo the full force of the storm slammed into the boys. It became impossible to run. Mawee stopped to huddle next to the road until the deluge let up.

Amee-nah didn't even see Mawee stop. He was blinded by the driving rain. What happened next happened so fast it stunned Amee-nah. A great crackling sound turned into a massive explosion of energy. A blinding flash of light filled the air. Amee-nah was knocked to the ground. His body quivered and shook. His hair crackled. He lay stunned for a few seconds.

As Amee-nah came to his senses, he checked his body. He seemed to be okay. The lightning strike had just missed him. The bewildered boy pulled himself to a standing position. He shouted Mawee's name. There was no answer. He frantically screamed for his friend with still no answer. Where was Mawee? Why couldn't he answer?

Amee-nah was in a state of shock. He knew something horrible must have happened. In his dazed condition Amee-nah began a search for his friend. Thunder and lightning and pouring rain continued.

His friend had to be close by. Over and over Amee-nah shouted Mawee's name. Fear gripped the boy with each passing second.

Amee-nah had just seen Mawee before the lightning struck. Now he was terrified by the thought of what may have happened to his friend. He shuddered to think that Mawee might have been killed. A sense of panic gripped Amee-nah.

Almost as quickly as the storm had hit, it passed the terrified boy. Now Amee-nah could see much farther. His eyes searched everywhere for any sign of Mawee.

Amee-nah heard his friend before he spotted him. Mawee lay next to a dwarf cedar tree calling Amee-nah's name. The boy dashed to his fallen friend who lay helplessly in the mud.

"Mawee! Are you all right? Are you hurt? What happened?" Amee-nah cried.

The fallen boy could hardly speak. Amee-nah gently lifted Mawee's head from the mud. With tears pouring down his cheeks, Amee-nah held his friend's head in his lap. He carefully wiped the mud from Mawee's face.

Amee-nah was confused. How could this be happening? Only minutes before, both boys were running down the road. Now everything had changed.

"Mawee, please be okay. Please don't die. I'm here to help you. Everything will be all right," Amee-nah sobbed as he looked at his best friend.

The next minutes seemed like hours. Amee-nah tried to get control of himself. He knew if he panicked he could never help his friend. *Calm down,* he told himself.

"Amee-nah," whispered Mawee. "I'm all right. I was just stunned. My right side feels numb, but I think I'm okay. Just let me rest a few minutes."

"Mawee, you're talking. I'll see if you are hurt," Amee-nah stammered.

Amee-nah used his shirt for a pillow under Mawee's head. On his hands and knees Amee-nah began to examine his friend for injuries. One look at Mawee's right foot made Amee-nah gasp. The bare foot was blackened. Blood was oozing from Mawee's heel. The lightning had struck the boy on his right side and traveled downward coming out

from his right heel. Amee-nah was devastated by the hideous appearance of the wound.

"Mawee, it's your foot. Your foot is bleeding a little," Amee-nah told his friend as calmly as possible. "I'll go for help. Will you be okay? I won't be gone long."

"Thank you, Amee-nah." Mawee murmured. "Sure, I'll be fine. I feel better. Hurry back."

Amee-nah breathed a sigh of relief. Now it was up to him. He felt a sudden calm. He was gaining control of himself. He slowly stood up next to Mawee. With one last look at his injured friend, Amee-nah turned and raced off at top speed. With his adrenaline pumping wildly, the determined boy sprinted down the road faster than he had ever dreamed he would run.

Amee-nah wouldn't remember much of this desperate run. He would cover the mile in a blur of speed. Two men building a new house had just come out as the rain was stopping. Amee-nah dashed up to them with the news of Mawee's tragic injuries. The men ran to their truck. With Amee-nah between them they drove off to rescue the fallen boy.

That night Amee-nah, Coach K, and Mawee's family sat in the waiting room at the Blackrock hospital. They talked softly as they waited for the latest news of Mawee's condition. Mawee's mother sat quietly most of the time. Her eyes were closed as she prayed for her son's recovery.

Finally the doctor came into the waiting room. He had great news. Mawee would recover completely. His right foot was badly burned but would heal. The doctor said Mawee was a very lucky young man. The lightning could have ended the boy's life. His was a brush with death.

After the doctor left, Mawee's mother gave Amee-nah a hug. "You saved our son's life. Thank you, Amee-nah. We love you," the boy's mother said softly.

"I didn't do much. Anyone could have done the same thing. Mawee is my best friend. I would have done anything to help him," Amee-nah stated sincerely.

"Amee-nah, you're great!" Coach K declared. "You kept your head. You acted fast. You were there when Mawee needed you most."

While Mawee's parents went in to visit their son, Amee-nah sat quietly in the waiting room in deep thought. Coach K left with a promise to return soon for a visit.

The longer Amee-nah sat there, the more the reality of the accident became clear. Mawee would not be able to run on his injured foot for weeks. He would have to miss the big race that he had trained so hard to win. Amee-nah knew his good friend would be the most disappointed person in all of Zuni. Now someone would have to run in Mawee's place. Amee-nah was sure Mawee's team wouldn't have a chance without their best racer. The boy wondered who would be picked to take Mawee's place.

9

A Last Effort

Mawee's father disturbed Amee-nah's thoughts when he came from Mawee's room. He invited the boy to come in to see Mawee.

As Amee-nah came through the door, Mawee broke into a big smile. Mawee's foot was bandaged with thick white gauze. It rested on a pillow slightly elevated.

"Hi, Amee-nah. Thanks for coming." Mawee tried to sound cheerful.

"Boy, am I glad to see you!" Amee-nah answered. "The doctor says you will heal perfectly. I never thought you would end up with a bad foot. I thought I was the only one who was that lucky," Amee-nah kidded.

"Yeah, it's the pits, but I'm sure glad you were there. I guess I'm lucky to be alive. I can't believe how fast you covered that mile to the men and their truck. Thanks, old friend, for getting help so fast," Mawee stated with gratitude.

"It was nothing. I can't even remember that run. I must have been in a trance," Amee-nah confessed.

"Well, Amee-nah, I won't be running in the stick race this weekend. I'll hate to miss the race. Now I have to pick a substitute. It's up to me."

"That should be easy. There are lots of great runners to pick from. Have you picked someone yet?" Amee-nah asked. "The race is only five days away."

"Yes, I have a great runner all picked out. He just finished running a mile in record-breaking time. Amee-nah, I want you to run for me," Mawee declared.

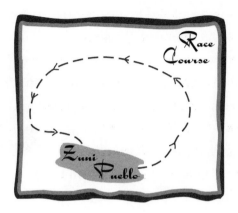

Amee-nah was shocked. Had he heard Mawee's words correctly? Was his friend kidding? He couldn't mean it. How could Mawee pick someone who had never run a stick race in his life?

"You're kidding, Mawee. Me? Me run in the race for you? Everyone . . . everyone will laugh," Amee-nah stammered.

"Let 'em laugh," Mawee blurted. "You're the one who raced that record mile to save me. You can kick the stick as well as anyone. No one wants to run more than you. No one wants to win more than you. There isn't anyone else for me. I'll be at the fin-

ish line when you and my team cross it. We'll celebrate the championship together!"

"I'll be there, too," a voice shouted from the hall-
way. Coach K came trotting into the room. "Mawee,
I came back as fast as I could. I've been praying for
you. Amee-nah, Mawee made a great choice. You
will run and make us all proud of you, win or lose. I
know you'll give it everything you have!"

Amee-nah didn't know what to say. Things had
happened so fast his mind was numb. The boy took
a deep breath.

"Mawee, if you're sure you want me to run, I
promise I'll do my best," Amee-nah said weakly.

As Amee-nah headed home late that evening,
his mind was full of thoughts about all that had
happened in such a short time. The boy's mother
had already stopped at the hospital to hear about
Mawee. When Amee-nah told his mother that
Mawee wanted him to run in the stick race, she
said something he would remember the rest of
his life.

"Son, when a good friend needs you and you're there to help, no matter what you do, all will turn out well."

The next day Amee-nah's practice with Mawee's team began. They practiced from after school until dark. At first Amee-nah thought his three teammates were disappointed to have him on their team. Before this first practice ended these same three boys would be impressed with how good Amee-nah was. Still, each of the three boys thought their chances of winning were gone. How could they ever win with their best runner out with a burned foot? Oh, well, they would run anyway.

Practice for three days was grueling. Amee-nah gave it everything he had. Each day he stopped by Mawee's house for a visit. Each day Mawee told Amee-nah he knew their team would win the race. Mawee told Amee-nah to think about the finish line. Mawee said he could see Amee-nah crossing the line ahead of the other team. "See yourself winning," Mawee told Amee-nah. "You can win."

The day of the big race finally came. The weather was perfect. Hundreds of people gathered early near the starting line. Many were talking about the bad luck suffered by Mawee, the finest racer on either team. Most people were willing to bet on the other team to beat Mawee's team easily. Without Mawee how could his team win? Boys who had teased Amee-nah for years by calling him names laughed when they heard that Mawee had picked Amee-nah to run for him.

"What a joke!" one boy laughed. "Amee-nah? What a joke!"

The days before the race had been anxious days for Amee-nah. His stomach was full of butterflies. He stayed away from everyone except his teammates. The four boys ate their paper bread and talked about the coming race. Amee-nah's teammates gave him some great tips on how to work as a team. They told him they would do most of the kicking. He would be counted on to be there when he was needed.

Amee-nah could tell the three boys were going to try to win the race mostly by themselves. They were nice about it, but Amee-nah was sure they were not expecting too much help from him.

The crowd was huge at race time. A loud cheer broke out when last year's winning team came up to the starting line. John, Paul, and their two team- mates were sweating from their warm-up runs. Their bodies glistened in the sun. They were big, strong runners. People in the crowd began chanting their names over and over.

As Amee-nah and his team jogged up to the start, a few cheers went up from their fans. People were quietly talking about how sure they were that Mawee's team had no chance without him.

Amee-nah knew everyone was staring at him. He hardly knew where to look. He was very tense. His stomach was doing flipflops. Then his eyes met with Mawee's. He stood on one foot with the help of his crutches. Coach K, Mawee's mother and father, and Amee-nah's mother stood next to the injured boy.

"Hey, Amee-nah! You look great!" he yelled. "I know you're gonna run a super race. The other guys say they're really glad you're running with them. Go get 'em, partner. We'll be here to see the great victory. Your dad will be looking down and clapping for you! I can see you guys crossing the line with a great win!"

"I'll do my best," Amee-nah promised with a trembling voice.

The two teams were called to line up. A horse and rider would ride next to each team. As long as the horses were in view, the people could tell which team was in the lead. When the horses couldn't be seen, spotters on the hillsides would signal to the crowd to let them know who was ahead. For the first part of the race, young Zuni boys would run along with the racers, keeping a short distance away. They would scream encouragement to their favorite team.

The starter was a man honored to be chosen for his important job. He ordered the racers to take their places. He explained the familiar rules of the stick race. Amee-nah listened carefully. At the same time he could almost hear his heart pounding in his chest. His excitement was practically unbearable.

The starter raised his beautifully decorated starting pole high into the air. He held it high for a few seconds. Everyone was silent. Down it came. The racers were off and running. Amee-nah felt a great relief to finally be into the race. It was the beginning of an exhausting twenty-five miles to the finish line.

Amee-nah would not remember much of the first half of the race. He was hit by a burning side ache. For a few minutes the pain was so great that he felt like dropping out. Somehow the boy kept running. The ache finally disappeared.

The first part of the race was mostly uphill on a narrow rough road. Amee-nah was keeping up with no trouble, but he hardly ever had a chance to kick the stick. His teammates were in charge. Both teams seemed to be taking turns being ahead. They were evenly matched so far.

Then a little past the halfway mark, one runner from each team accidentally collided and crashed to the rocky ground. Both teams lost a racer in this mishap. Now it was three against three.

Instantly Amee-nah realized he would be needed more than ever. Now he had many more chances to send the stick flying. In a short time he would be needed even more.

Three miles after the first accident one of Amee-nah's teammates hit a loose rock. Down he went with a badly sprained ankle. He was out of the race with eight long miles to go.

Now there were only two on Amee-nah's team. It was two against three to the finish. Amee-nah found himself relaying the stick on and on with his only remaining teammate.

Word was brought to the crowd that the teams were still neck and neck. The crowd was shocked to hear that Amee-nah was still running. They could hardly believe it. Some even thought there must be some mistake.

The hundreds of onlookers strained their eyes to catch sight of the approaching runners. Spotters kept racing back with the latest reports. Amee-nah and his partner were falling behind. They already trailed by twenty yards.

Three miles out the horseback riders could be seen. They were practically side by side. Surprisingly Amee-nah and his teammate had made a dramatic comeback. The crowd was astounded. How could these two runners be staying with three of the strongest runners in all of Zuni? How could a boy who had never run a race still be in the race and challenging such powerful runners? No one could understand these unbelievable events.

Charging down the dusty road, Amee-nah and his partner were working in perfect harmony. Their stick seemed to land in the best possible positions. Their kicks were catching the best wind gusts.

As the two teams reached the last quarter mile, the crowd was roaring. Amee-nah could hear nothing. He concentrated a hundred percent on his task. He felt a strange calmness and a continued surge of energy.

In the last two hundred yards Amee-nah and his partner fell a few yards behind. Amee-nah noticed a look of disappointment on his teammate's face.

No! It's not over. We're not giving up now! Amee-nah cried to himself.

With his next kick, Amee-nah sent their stick flying like an arrow from a bowstring. His partner timed its landing perfectly and made his own powerful kick. With these two outstanding moves, the two boys pulled back even with their three opponents. Now it was again neck and neck with the finish line in sight.

After one more good kick by Amee-nah, his partner desperately tried to get to the stick as it landed. The anxious boy stumbled in a dip in the road and went sprawling. He was out of the race! Now it was Amee-nah alone for the last hundred yards.

Amee-nah felt a sudden feeling of helplessness. He was alone. It seemed almost too much for any boy to handle.

Instantly Amee-nah recalled Mawee's words, "We'll be here to celebrate your victory. Your dad will be looking down and clapping for you." These words rang in Amee-nah's mind. He could already see himself crossing the finish line. With all his final reserves of energy the boy launched one final charge to the finish line.

He closed the gap with the runners ahead of him. The crowd was going wild. None of them could believe what they were witnessing. Could it really be that three powerful runners were being challenged by a single runner who had never run in a stick race in his life?

Mawee was up on his crutches shrieking at the top of his lungs. Coach K was jumping up and down and screaming Amee-nah's name over and over. Amee-nah's mother had lost her voice shouting for her son.

In the final twenty yards the teams' two sticks landed only three feet apart. Amee-nah and John reached their sticks at exactly the same time. John, in a desperate effort to beat Amee-nah to the next kick, overran his stick. This split-second slip gave Amee-nah the chance he needed.

Amee-nah timed his stop perfectly. Like he had seen Mawee do many times, the boy scooped up the stick with almost no stop at all. The stick seemed to have wings. It sailed high and far, landing within reach of the finish line.

Like a robot Amee-nah cruised to the fallen stick. Gasping for every breath the boy charged to his stick. With one final effort Amee-nah sent his stick sailing across the finish line where it landed at Mawee's feet. With John right on his heels, Amee-nah sprinted across the finish line. The stunned crowd exploded with cheers of amazement.

Before Amee-nah's legs caved in, Coach K grabbed the boy. Now the crowd went wild. Never had anyone witnessed such a close finish to a stick race. After twenty-five miles of endurance racing, only a few tenths of a second made the difference.

Coach K literally held Amee-nah upright. He kept Amee-nah walking. The coach knew severe cramps could hit the boy after his body had gone through such a demanding race. After he could stand without Coach K's help, Uncle James gave the boy some water to sip.

As the cheering crowd began to quiet down a little, Coach K began clapping. One by one others joined in. The clapping grew louder and louder.

Amee-nah finally began to realize what had happened. His team had won. The clapping brought a smile to his face. The impossible had happened. As weak as he felt, Amee-nah managed to walk over to Mawee. Neither boy could speak. They grabbed each other in a great bear hug with the clapping ringing in their ears.

Finally Coach K picked up the crutches Mawee had dropped. He handed them to the boy who was grinning from ear to ear.

"Amee-nah, you did it! You're the greatest! Now where are the people who said our team had no chance? Now they can pay up those bets they made! I know your dad can hear the clapping. Amee-nah, you're the greatest!" he bubbled.

"He's right!" Coach K shouted. "You ran a fantastic race! No one will call you Amee-nah again! Lazy is a name you never deserved!"

"He's right," a deep voice boomed. "Even I didn't think you could have done what I just witnessed here today."

It was Dr. Mike. The good doctor had arrived when the race was half over. Coach K had called him when Amee-nah was picked to run. On his way to

California to see relatives, Dr. Mike decided to pay a visit to his young patient. He arrived just in time.

The end of the race was followed by a great celebration. For years to come the story of Amee-nah's great determination would be told over and over again. Old Joshua thanked Amee-nah for giving him another great tale to tell.

10

Epilogue

As Amee-nah and Mawee hugged each other standing near the finish line, their joy was so great they were unaware of all the cheers sounding about them. They didn't hear everyone jabbering in amazement about Amee-nah's astounding feat.

When the excitement finally died down, the winning racers and their families gathered for a great celebration. Coack K and Dr. Mike were guests of

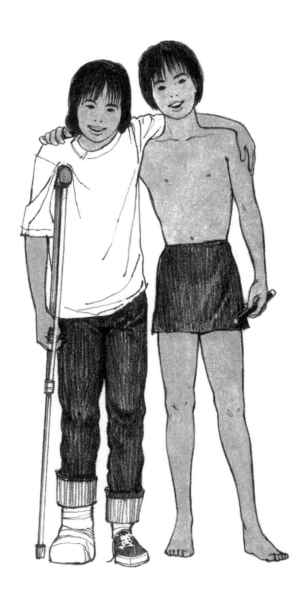

honor along with the winning racers. At that party Mawee looked at Amee-nah and spoke proudly.

"Amee-nah, you told me you sort of like your nickname, but remember it means lazy. Lazy doesn't fit you one bit. It never did. From now on I'm calling you by your real name. Nathan is a great name for you. Coach K says Nathan means a gift from God. Nathan, you are a gift to me. You're a super friend. Get used to your real name. It's the only one I'm going to use," declared Mawee.

So it was. The name *Amee-nah* would fade away. Nathan and Mawee would become even closer friends. At the same party Nathan and his mother talked to Coach K about Nathan's desire to go to the mission school. Coach K said he could make the arrangements for Nathan to start at the school in September.

With great excitement Nathan joined Mawee for the new school year at the mission school. Mawee's foot had healed perfectly. The two boys worked hard in their studies and had many more adventures at sheep camp. When one of Mawee's teammates moved away, Nathan joined the stickracing team and went on to win many more races.

On December 7, 1941, the United States entered World War II after the surprise bombing of Pearl Harbor by Japan. Nathan was a teenager during this horrible war. His heart was broken when the news came that Uncle James had lost his life. It happened on June 6, 1943, on the Omaha Beach during the Normandy invasion. A gold star was hung in the window of Uncle James' home to mark his sacrifice. Many more gold stars were hung in Zuni windows as more and more young men gave their lives for their country. Along with people from coast to coast Nathan learned the high cost of freedom.

Nathan's hard work in school earned him a scholarship to college. Like Dr. Mike, Nathan overcame his disability and went on to become a fine college athlete. During the summer months Nathan earned money as a forest firefighter. His college career was interrupted by his service as a marine in the Korean War. Nathan and Mawee served in the same unit. Both were decorated for bravery when their unit turned back an attack on their position by overwhelming numbers of Chinese troops.

After the war Nathan finished his college education and went on to become a veterinarian. Mawee and Nathan married twin sisters and raised families of their own. They stayed close to Coach K and the mission school. They remembered the day they attended the funeral of old Joshua. They continued to share the old shepherd's stories with their own children.

All through his life Nathan thought about his father. Even as an adult the man once called Amee-nah would hear the clapping he had heard as a young boy. Everyday in his prayers, Nathan gave thanks for his father and his mother. His thanksgiving list always included Mawee, Coach K, Dr. Mike, Old Joshua, and especially Uncle James.

Author Ken Thomasma is a professional storyteller and writing workshop leader living in Jackson Hole, Wyoming. *Amee-Nah* is the seventh book in his series "Amazing Indian Children."

Michigan artist Jack Brouwer is a signature member of the American Watercolor Society, the National Watercolor Society, and the Midwest Watercolor Society.